# WHAT HAPPENED HERE?

# VIKING STREET

## Marilyn Tolhurst

Photographs by Maggie Murray
Illustrations by Gillian Clements

## Contents

## A & C BLACK · LONDON

# Who lived here?

This book is about a street in York called Coppergate. The picture shows Coppergate as it might have looked 1000 years ago when the Vikings lived there.

The Vikings attacked York on 1 November 866 and captured the city. Shortly after, Viking settlers and their families moved in, setting up homes and workshops. At that time, York was called Eoforwik. The Vikings changed the city's name to suit their own language. They called it Jorvik from which we get our modern name, York. Jorvik became a Viking stronghold which was ruled by Viking kings for the next 80 years.

In 1976, a factory in Coppergate was knocked down. This gave archaeologists a chance to excavate the site and discover what lay beneath the modern street. They found the remains of several Viking houses and many clues to the Viking way of life.

The children in this book wanted to find out what life was like in Coppergate in Viking times. They began their investigation at the Jorvik Viking Centre in York.

wood turner

combmaker

After excavating the remains of the houses in Coppergate, archaeologists reconstructed them. They built an exact copy of Viking Coppergate and filled the houses with the things they might have contained 1000 years ago. Today you can visit the site which is now a museum of Viking life in York.

jeweller

Coppergate

blacksmith

storage pots and jars

straw thatch

heather bedding

central hearth

woven blanket

3

# How do we know about the Viking street?

Everything the archaeologists found during the excavation at Coppergate, from the iron helmet to the smallest rat bone, was a clue to the way the Vikings in York lived 1000 years ago. Archaeologists pieced these clues together to get a picture of what life was like in Viking Coppergate.

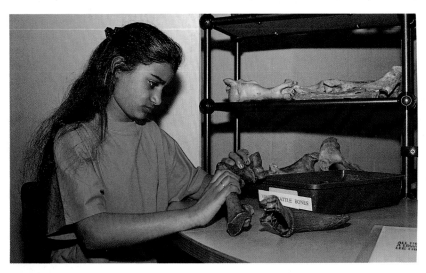

Archaeologists look at every object in great detail. This girl sorted through Viking cattle bones at the Archaeological Resource Centre in York. She compared the size of old bones with modern ones. She discovered that Viking cows were much smaller than cows today.

## Viking writing

Other clues about the Vikings have come from their stories and their pictures. The saga of *Egil's Head Ransom* (see page 29) tells us a great deal about raiding and fighting. *The Anglo-Saxon Chronicle*, a history book written by monks at the time, tells us how people in England felt about Viking raids.

## Other Viking remains

Archaeologists have excavated many other Viking sites. The remains of buildings, weapons, coins, jewellery and clothing found at these places have all added to our picture of Viking life. Two magnificent ship burials found in Norway gave historians important evidence about the way the Vikings built and sailed their ships.

Objects such as household pots and carvings of gods found at Viking sites gave clues about the places the Vikings sailed to, and the goods they traded.

▲ This cart is a faithful copy of one found in a rich Viking grave in Norway. Reconstructions like this can tell us a lot about the technology of the time. The man is dressed in reproduction Viking clothes. The clothes were made using the evidence of remains which have been found at Viking burial sites.

◄ The Coppergate dig in process. Most of the Viking houses were found at the top of the site near the main road. Rubbish pits and lavatories were in the yards behind. Many of the houses had been rebuilt several times. They were excavated layer by layer and all the thousands of finds were carefully cleaned and labelled.

# Time-lines

The first time-line shows some of the important events which took place during Viking times. The second time-line shows some of the important events in the history of Jorvik, up to the present day.

**Main events, ideas and inventions**

AD 793

The Vikings live in troubled and lawless times after the fall of the Roman Empire. Some people later called this time the Dark Ages. Very little is written about it by people living at the time. Many of the technical advances of the Romans are forgotten.

**AD 793** The first Viking raid on England. Vikings plunder the Northumbrian monastery of Lindisfarne.

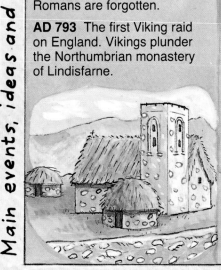

**AD 800** Viking raids on England increase.

The Vikings are successful raiders and explorers mostly because of their longships.

These are the fastest ships afloat and give the Vikings a great advantage over their enemies. Vikings rule the seas.

**AD 865** A great Viking army lands in East Anglia.

The Vikings worship a family of gods led by Odin and his son Thor. They believe that men who die in battle go straight to heaven. This makes them fearless warriors.

The Vikings eventually occupy most of eastern England. They establish a Viking kingdom in York.

**Events at Jorvik**

AD 866

**AD 866** A great Viking army attacks and captures York.

**AD 867** King Aelle attacks the Vikings near York. During the battle Aelle and many of his Saxon soldiers are killed. The Vikings take control of York and rename it Jorvik, which is a Viking word for wild boar creek.

**AD 876** Viking settlers, led by Halfdan, move into York. Halfdan becomes the first Viking king of Northumbria.

**AD 927** The powerful Anglo-Saxon leader, Athelstan, the grandson of Alfred the Great, captures York and holds it until 939.

**AD 939** The English and the Vikings struggle for control of York.

AD 1100

**AD 886** The Saxon king Alfred the Great makes war with the Vikings and tries to win back parts of England.

England is divided into two kingdoms, one ruled by the English, and the other ruled by the Vikings and known as the Danelaw.

**AD 900** The Vikings become great traders. They make contact with many other peoples in Europe and beyond and trade with them. They begin to make laws and collect taxes.

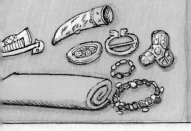

**AD 909** King Alfred's son and daughter win control of all of England except the Viking kingdom of Northumbria.

**AD 1000** Christian missionaries preach in Viking lands. Christianity gradually replaces their old pagan beliefs.

**AD 1016–35** King Cnut the Great rules a large kingdom which includes Norway, Denmark and most of Britain. He is the last Viking king of England.

**AD 1066** The English king Harold defeats the Viking leader, Harald Hardrada (Hard-Ruler) at the battle of Stamford Bridge. King Harold is himself beaten by the Normans under their leader Duke William at the battle of Hastings. William the Conqueror is crowned King William I of England.

**AD 1100** Viking power starts to fade although their language, arts and crafts continue to be important in all the lands they have conquered.

1984

**AD 954** Eric Bloodaxe, the last Viking king of York, is defeated and thrown out of the city.

**AD 1068** King William I takes control of England and builds castles in York.

**1975** An old sweet factory in Coppergate is demolished to make way for new building. A team of archaeologists takes the opportunity to excavate the site. They discover the remains of Viking houses under the street. They spend the next five years investigating the site and recording their findings.

**1984** The Viking houses in Coppergate are reconstructed. The whole site is turned into a museum where visitors can see for themselves what Viking life in York was like a thousand years ago.

# Who were the Vikings?

The Vikings were sometimes known as Norse or Northmen. They came from Scandinavia, from the countries now called Denmark, Sweden and Norway. To go 'a-viking' meant to be a pirate, and was how the Northmen described the swift, fierce raids they made.

Viking raids on England began in 793. In that year a band of Viking warriors landed from their longships to attack and plunder the monastery at Lindisfarne. Such attacks became common over the next 50 years and were usually so sudden that defence was almost impossible. Most raiding took place during the spring and summer which became known as the 'Viking season'. In autumn and winter the raiders returned home, taking anything valuable such as furs, silver and gold with them.

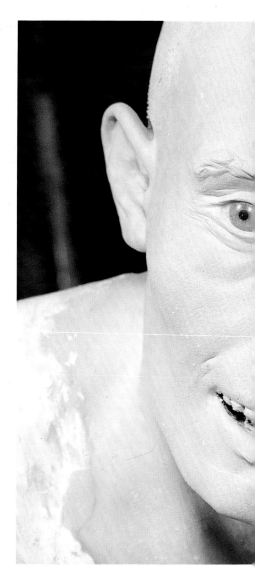

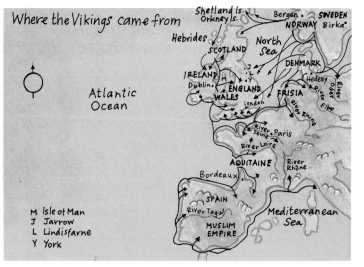

Where the Vikings came from

- M Isle of Man
- J Jarrow
- L Lindisfarne
- Y York

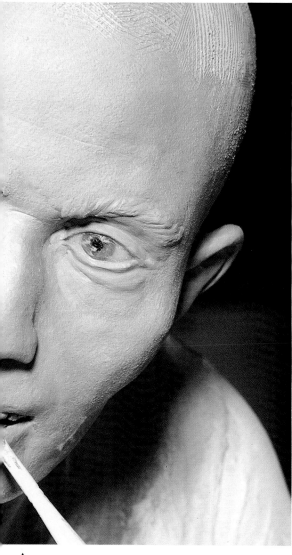

The Vikings were skilled craftworkers as well as fierce fighters. This man, dressed in replica Viking clothes, is making a spearhead using a charcoal forge and copies of Viking tools. The Vikings made beautiful jewellery for trading as well as strong weapons. Viking craftworkers and traders made York into a great trading centre.

▲
In 1990 scientists used the latest laser and computer technology to reconstruct this face from a Viking skull found in York. For the first time in a thousand years it is possible to look at the likeness of a real Viking.

This young man lives in modern York. He may be descended from the Vikings. By looking at Viking skeletons, archaeologists have found that, thanks to our better diet and modern medical care, we are probably taller and healthier than Vikings of the same age.

In 865 a huge army of Vikings arrived in East Anglia to seize not only gold, but land. The Vikings fought their way northwards to York. They captured the city and the whole kingdom of Northumbria. The Vikings struggled for power with the English for over a hundred years. In 1016 Viking King Cnut became king of England.

# Hearth and home

The children looked inside a reconstructed house at the Jorvik Viking Centre. They were surprised how cramped it was inside the house which was shared by parents, children, aunts, uncles and grandparents. There were no upstairs rooms at all. Downstairs there was just one room where the Viking family ate, slept, worked and entertained their friends. The huge fireplace, edged with stones, was the centre of family life.

The room was dark and smoky with pots, pans, buckets and sacks crammed in every corner and even hanging from the rafters. Outside in the back yard there was a well, a storage pit, a rubbish pit and a cess pit for the lavatory. Chickens and geese scratched about in the rubbish.

This reconstructed Viking house shows all the clutter of everyday life. The children noticed that there was very little furniture, just earth-filled benches for sitting and sleeping on. In spite of this they thought the room looked quite cosy.

The children learned that Vikings made their houses out of wooden posts with wicker panels filling the gaps. The walls were covered with sticky clay, called daub, to keep the wind out. The Vikings thatched the roofs and made the floors from beaten earth.

Anything valuable in a Viking home, such as jewellery, fine fabric or furs, might have been locked up in a chest like this. A number of Viking 'barrel padlocks' were found at the Coppergate site. This boy is trying to work out how to open one. Can you see how it is done by looking at the drawing?

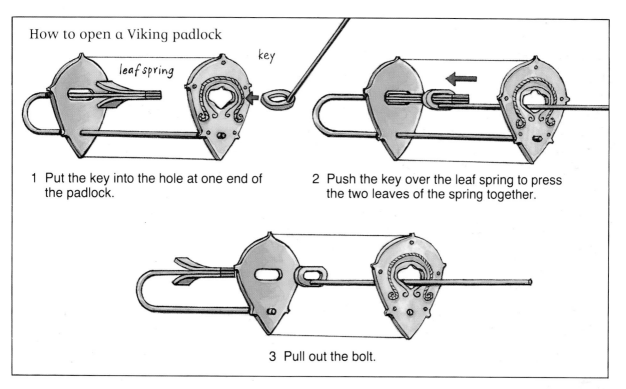

How to open a Viking padlock

leaf spring

key

1 Put the key into the hole at one end of the padlock.

2 Push the key over the leaf spring to press the two leaves of the spring together.

3 Pull out the bolt.

Viking women needed many skills to run their homes. They had to grind corn, make dough and beer, and salt down food for the winter. They also spun and wove cloth, made and mended garments, minded children, and tended the sick. Viking children probably had to help with fetching water and collecting wood for the fire.

# Getting dressed

We know something about Viking dress from the pictures the Vikings drew and the carvings they made. Viking men usually wore woollen tunics, loose trousers, linen shirts, and cloaks for extra warmth. Viking women wore tunics or aprons held up with straps over long, pleated linen dresses.

Viking women liked bright colours and often decorated their clothes with handwoven braid. They wore their hair plaited or tied up at the back, sometimes held in place by headbands. Everyone who could afford it wore jewellery.

The children tried on some Viking clothes. This girl thought that clothes made of linen and wool were warm and comfortable. The boy found that chainmail and a helmet were heavy and clumsy to wear.

From scraps of clothing found by archaeologists we know that the Vikings made most of their clothes from linen or wool. They spun their own yarn and wove their own cloth. Many Viking families owned a wooden loom that was stored against a wall when not in use.

The Vikings dyed the cloth in vats outside in their back yards. They used various plants to give colour, including woad for blue and weld for yellow. They cut the finished cloth with iron shears to make clothes.

Many Vikings also made their own leather caps, belts and shoes. Viking writings tell us that the Vikings bought expensive silks and furs at the market from merchants who travelled to foreign countries.

▲

The boys tried weaving cloth on a replica of a Viking loom. Heavy clay weights keep the vertical or warp threads tight. The weaver uses a huge wooden needle called a shuttle to weave the cloth. We know from a woollen sock found at Coppergate that the Vikings also knitted. Their knitting, which was called 'naalebinding', was rather like sewing. The knitter used a thick threaded needle to sew the wool in continuous loops.

Many leather items were preserved ▶ in the damp soil at Coppergate. This pair of shoes was copied from an original Viking shoe found at the site. It had leather thongs for laces. The girl who tried this pair said that they felt very comfortable.

# Food and drink

We know from seeds, nut shells, bones and other remains found at Coppergate that the Vikings who lived there ate many different foods during the year. Around the edge of these pages are some of the foods the Vikings ate. In autumn when the crops were gathered and the cattle slaughtered, the Vikings feasted.

But food was not easy to store. Meat went bad quickly unless it was salted or smoked for the winter. During colder weather, when food was scarce, the Vikings collected whatever they could. In early spring, when supplies were low and not much was growing, people often went hungry.

The Vikings ground grains into flour using handmills called querns. Each quern was made of two stones. The user poured grain into a hole at the top of the quern. The children turned the handle of this Viking quern to make the top stone rub against the bottom stone. The stones ground the grain into flour which trickled out at the sides.

The Vikings cooked their food over a fire and ate it from wooden bowls using spoons and knives. Pork, beef and mutton were favourite meats, but we know from bones found in rubbish pits that the Vikings ate chickens, ducks, hares and wild birds.

They also ate vegetables including carrots, parsnips and celery. They enjoyed fruit such as apples, plums and cherries, and sweetened their food with honey. They washed their meals down with weak, homemade beer.

The children learned that the Vikings wasted nothing. They tanned the skins of animals to make leather, and used animal horns to make drinking cups. They turned bones into toggles, spoons and combs and even used tiny bird bones to make needles.

These boys picked out fish bones from remains found in a Viking rubbish pit. They discovered that the Vikings of York ate at least twenty different kinds of fish.

This girl discovered that the curved shape of a Viking drinking horn makes it awkward to use. Air or liquid can get trapped inside the horn, making it hard to drink from.

# Keeping clean

In Viking times, Coppergate must have been a very dirty and smelly street. The Vikings did not know about germs so they did not take much care with their rubbish.

Archaeologists discovered that the Vikings littered their floors with food scraps and threw their slops outside. The alleys between the houses were full of mud and animal droppings. Mice and black rats scuttled in and out of the houses.

These children discovered that carrying a wooden bucket full of water is no easy task. They thought this might have been one of the reasons why Vikings did not bath very often.

The Vikings used lavatories that were just holes in the yards outside their houses. The wells they used for drinking water were often close to lavatory and rubbish pits and must have been polluted by all the filth around. Coppergate swarmed with flies in summertime. The children thought that sickness and stomach-ache must have been very common among the Vikings.

We know from early writings that the Vikings knew little about what made people ill. They could cure some illnesses with homemade herbal medicines. But they could do little to help people with serious diseases, bad wounds or who were in great pain.

It is not surprising that many Vikings died young. From the evidence of Viking skeletons we know that most Vikings probably died before the age of 60. Many women died before the age of 35 giving birth to their babies. Children often died from diseases that are easy to cure today.

This plank with a circular hole in it is a Viking lavatory seat. It was discovered at the bottom of an old cess pit. The Vikings had no lavatory paper. They used moss instead.

The excavation of remains in this rubbish pit at Jorvik provided archaeologists with important evidence about what the Vikings ate and the diseases they suffered from.

17

# The market

The name Coppergate, which comes from 'koppr', the old Norse word for cup, means the street of the cupmakers. Viking remains found at the site are evidence that many people who lived in the street were woodturners.

They made cups and bowls in the yards behind their houses and sold them in the market. They used wood to make other household items such as spoons, knife handles, buckets and barrels.

▲
There has been a market in York for over 1000 years. This girl is buying a washing-up bowl at a modern market stall.

This market stall has been ▶ reconstructed at the Jorvik Viking Centre. In Coppergate each craftworker had a stall in the market near his or her house. The Vikings of York could buy their buckets straight from the people who made them.

These are modern copies of bone and antler goods which the Vikings of Coppergate made and used. How many items can you name?

Other craftworkers made beautiful objects out of bone such as buckles, strap ends, sword handles and musical pipes. So many deer antler combs were found in Coppergate that it seems likely the street contained a workshop which made combs to be sold abroad.

Coppergate leatherworkers left behind the remains of leather boots, shoes and beautifully decorated belts. Blacksmiths made iron goods including nails, horseshoes, padlocks and swords. Jewellers made bronze and jewelled rings, cloak pins and brooches. The 10,000 people living in York provided plenty of custom for the craftworkers.

# A ship comes in

The Vikings were great seafarers. Even without the help of maps and compasses, they found their way across great oceans, steering only by the sun and stars. They were famous for their longships which were fast and deadly, each one powered by many oars and a sail. Longships were built for speed and to carry fighting men on raiding expeditions.

Part of an iron decoration on the door of Stillingfleet Church in North Yorkshire shows the shape of a Viking longship.

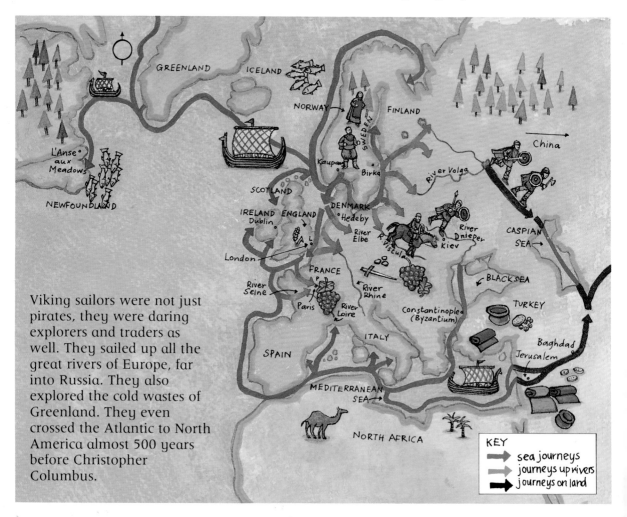

Viking sailors were not just pirates, they were daring explorers and traders as well. They sailed up all the great rivers of Europe, far into Russia. They also explored the cold wastes of Greenland. They even crossed the Atlantic to North America almost 500 years before Christopher Columbus.

KEY
→ sea journeys
→ journeys up rivers
→ journeys on land

This is what we think a Viking merchant ship looked like. The sail, shown rolled up here, was used at sea. The oars were used to propel the ship into land. We know from Viking writings that it took a ship like this about two weeks to sail from Norway to York.

York was a busy international trading port in Viking times. Viking merchant ships were shallow and fairly flat-bottomed so they could sail up rivers and land almost anywhere. Viking traders often used pack ponies to carry their cargoes from ship to shore.

Viking merchant ships were broader and slower than longships so they could carry a lot more cargo. The cargoes they brought to York came from ports all over Scandinavia, Russia and Europe. The Vikings of Coppergate often waited at the dock to see what luxuries the latest merchant ship had brought.

# Foreign trade

The Vikings set up trading posts wherever they sailed. The children learned that 1000 years ago York was the most important trading centre in England after London. Viking ships brought furs, silk, glass, wax, amber, silver, swords, pottery, fine wines and slaves to Jorvik.

Archaeologists have discovered many clues in Coppergate which show how far Viking traders travelled. They found walrus ivory brought from Norway; soapstone pots from the Shetland Islands; quernstones from Germany; cowrie shells from the Red Sea; amber from the Baltic and silk from the eastern Mediterranean. There was even a coin from Arabia.

The Vikings exchanged many of their goods by bartering or swapping, but they did buy some things with money. York had its own mint where local moneyers made silver pennies on behalf of the king. Many coins have been found in York either lost or buried in hoards which were never collected by their owners.

A silver penny like the ones made in York, showing the raven of the Viking god, Odin.

These children tried out the Viking method of minting a coin. They each placed a blank piece of silver between two halves of an engraved coin die, then bashed the die with a hammer to make a bright new penny.

▼ This is the reconstructed coin die which the children used.

# Fun and games

The Vikings liked to spend their free time in sport and play. We know from Viking stories and sagas that they enjoyed wrestling and games of strength. The children also discovered that a number of bone dice were found at Coppergate, telling them that games of chance were popular.

Viking dice made from bone.

These children discovered that playing hnefatafl is almost as difficult as pronouncing the name!

The Vikings may have spent many winter evenings round the fire playing hnefatafl (pronounced neffa-taffle) which was a game of skill something like draughts or chess. Each player had an army of bone pieces to move across the board. The aim was to surround an opponent's king and stop him getting to the corners.

A Viking boot and bone skate found in Coppergate. In winter time, when the streets were full of icy mud, it was probably quicker to skate down a frozen river than to walk down a road.

Skating was one of the Vikings' favourite winter pastimes. It was also a very practical way of travelling in very cold weather. The Vikings made their ice skates from bones, flattened and polished underneath. The skaters tied the skates on round their ankles. They probably used a pole something like a ski stick to push themselves along.

# Language and learning

The Vikings of Coppergate spoke a Scandinavian language called Old Norse. It was something like the Old English which was spoken by the Anglo-Saxons who lived in York before the Vikings came. There were probably some Old English speakers still living in the city in Viking times. Other inhabitants may have spoken Celtic, an even earlier language.

The English we speak today has bits of all these languages in it. We use many Viking words today without knowing it. Some of them begin with 'sk' such as skin, sky, skirt and skill. But there are also many others. When you use the words wish, want, root, same, wrong, flat, tight, freckles and awkward, you are speaking Viking!

Many street names in York survive ▶ from Viking times. Some of them end in the Old Norse word 'gate' or 'gata' which meant road or street rather than opening or entrance as it does today.

▲
A Viking alphabet is called a 'futhark' after the first sounds it contains. Not all Vikings used the same alphabet. The one shown here is a Norwegian futhark. It has only 16 runes or letters. This could make it difficult to spell some words. Can you work out which sounds found in our alphabet are missing from this futhark?

The Viking alphabet was made up of letters called runes. Few Vikings could read or write but when they needed to send a message, they asked a rune master to carve the letters on a piece of wood. Each rune was made up of straight lines because these were easier to carve than curved ones. There were no capital letters and very few punctuation marks, so messages had to be fairly simple.

▲ These children tried to read runic messages carved on pieces of wood called rune sticks. The Vikings may have believed that runes had magical powers. They sometimes used them to write down magic spells.

◄ Runes may have been designed for carving on wood, but they are also found on bone, metal and stone. This runic inscription carved on a stone in Sweden was put up in honour of a man called Ali and tells how he raided England and brought back gold.

# Stories and music

The Vikings loved stories, poems and riddles. A good storyteller was welcome anywhere. He was called a skald, and the stories he told were called sagas. Most sagas were tales of adventure and battle. Only a few of them were written down. Most were memorised and passed on from skald to skald.

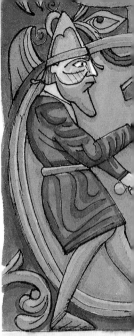

Thursday is named after Thor, the war son of Odin, whose wea was a great hamme

A modern skald in Viking costume entertains a group of children with an old tale of courage and daring. In Viking times a good skald was ...rded with gifts.

Wednesday is na after Wodin or Od was the father of all gods. He rode an eight-horse called Sleipni

One story told in York was so good that it saved a man's life. It was invented by a great poet called Egil Skallagrimsson. Egil was shipwrecked and taken prisoner by his enemy, Eric Bloodaxe, the Viking king of York. Egil was sentenced to death but, during the night, he wrote a long rhyming poem about the great deeds of the king. Eric Bloodaxe was so pleased that he let Egil go free and the poem afterwards was known as *Egil's Head Ransom*. The Vikings living in Coppergate must have heard this story while they sat by their fires.

A lot of Viking stories were about the old Norse gods who lived in the imaginary kingdom of Asgard. Many Vikings believed that if they died in battle they would join the gods in the great palace of Valhal. But we know that many of the Vikings of Coppergate did not believe in the old Norse gods. They must have been Christians because they were buried in Christian churchyards.

Tuesday is named after Tiw, the one-handed warrior, whose other hand was bitten off by the wolf, Fenfir.

We know, from the musical instruments that were found there, that the Vikings of Coppergate liked music. This set of panpipes was hollowed from a single piece of boxwood. It is still possible to get notes from the pipes but we have no way of knowing what tunes the Vikings played.

Friday is named after Freya, the wife of Odin, who made all living thing grow.

# How to find out more

## Visits

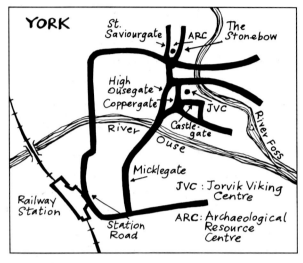

You can find out a great deal about the Vikings by visiting the Jorvik Viking Centre in Coppergate, York YO1 9WT. Tel: 01904 643211. Most of the objects shown in this book were excavated there. You can also visit the Archaeological Resource Centre in St Saviourgate, York. Tel: 01904 654324 if you want to find out about the way archaeologists work.

The Longship Trading Company, which also features in this book, can provide 'Living History' days where schools can experience Viking life by trying out replica clothes and tools of the period. Their address is: The Longship Trading Company Ltd, 342 Albion Street, Wall Heath, Kingswinford, West Midlands DY6 0JR. Tel: 01384 292237.

There are many Viking sites and museums throughout the country. The British Museum and the National Museum of Antiquities in Scotland both ⌐in important Viking material.

For information on suitable places to visit in your area contact:
English Heritage Education Service
Tel: 020 7973 3442/3
Historic Scotland
Tel: 0131 668 8600
The National Trust
Tel: 020 7222 9251

## Things to do

Here are some ideas for things to do which could help you to find out more about life in Viking times.

### Use runes to send messages

The runic alphabet on page 26 contains most of the sounds you need to spell words. You can use it to write your name in runes or to send secret messages.

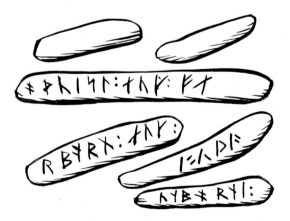

## Make a Viking helmet

You will need: some bendy cardboard (cereal packet card is ideal), a stapler, some tissue paper and glue.

Cut a strip of card about 6cm deep and fit it round your head so that it covers your eyes. Staple it together at the back. Cut out a piece at the front to clear your eyes.

Cut another strip of card and put it over your head. Staple it back and front to the first piece. Staple another piece of card side to side in the same way.

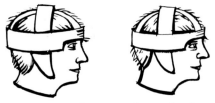

Make some ear flaps and staple them to the side to cover your ears.

Make a nose guard just big enough to cover your nose. Staple it to the front.

Glue strips of tissue paper onto the helmet until it is completely covered. Make sure you cover all the staples to stop them scratching. When the glue has dried, add another layer of tissue to give strength.

Once the helmet is dry, you could decorate it with runic patterns.

---

## Make some Viking hearth cakes

Ask an adult to help you.

The Vikings did not always use wheatflour for their baking. They often used other grains such as barley, oats and rye. Sometimes they used a mixture of wheat and rye called maslin. This recipe contains barleymeal and oatmeal which you can buy from healthfood shops.

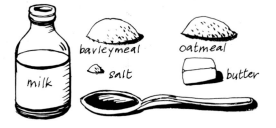

Mix together 2 tablespoons of barleymeal, 2 tablespoons of oatmeal and a pinch of salt in a bowl. Rub in 57g of butter. Add enough milk to make a dough that is firm but not sticky. Shape it into round flat cakes.

The Vikings would have baked their hearth cakes on hot stones by the fire, perhaps placing an upended cauldron over them to create a makeshift oven. You can bake your hearth cakes slowly on a griddle over the kitchen stove or even on a barbecue when the ashes have cooled a bit.

# Index

First paperback edition 2000

First published 1994 in hardback by
A & C.Black (Publishers) Limited
35 Bedford Row
London WC1R 4JH

ISBN 0-7136-5368-X

© 1994 A & C Black (Publishers) Limited

A CIP catalogue record for this book is available from the British Library.

Books in the series available in hardback:
Roman Fort
Tudor Farmhouse
Tudor Warship
Victorian Factory

Acknowledgements
The author and publishers would like to thank Dr Dominic Tweddle (Assistant Director of the York Archaeological Trust) and Katie Jones; the staff at the Jorvik Viking Centre, Coppergate, York especially Peter Greenwood; the staff and volunteers at the Archaeological Resource Centre, York especially Ruth Dass; all members of the Longship Trading Company; Bertie Tolhurst, Danny Milne, Rachel Harty, Kim Stannard, Josh and Miranda Punter and Jason Smith.

Photographs by Maggie Murray except for: pp3, 4/5 (middle), 8/9 (middle), 10, 17 both, 18 (bottom), 20, 24 (top), 25, 29
The Archaeological and Heritage Picture Library, York.

Filmset by Rowland Phototypesetting Ltd, Bury St Edmunds, Suffolk.

Printed and bound in Italy by L.E.G.O.